Disney's
American Frontier #14

LAWMEN
STORIES OF MEN WHO TAMED THE WEST

by Bryce Milligan
Illustrations by Charlie Shaw
Cover illustration by Daniel O'Leary

DISNEY PRESS
NEW YORK

FIRST EDITION
1   3   5   7   9   10   8   6   4   2

Library of Congress Catalog Card Number: 94-70797
ISBN: 0-7868-4006-4/0-7868-5005-1 (lib. bdg.)

Consultant: Tom Burks, Curator
Texas Rangers Hall of Fame and Museum, Waco, Texas

CONTENTS

INTRODUCTION

By the 1880s towns had sprouted up all across the American frontier. Many were settled by poor farmers who had moved west looking for cheap land. When gold was discovered in California in 1848, gold fever swept the nation. Prospectors hoping to strike it rich moved into the mountains by the thousands. Mining towns such as Yankee Hill, Colorado, sprang up almost overnight.

The most famous towns in the Old West were the cow towns. Several times each year thousands of cowboys from all over Texas, Colorado, Wyoming, and Montana would lead huge herds of cattle on long trips—known as cattle drives—to towns such as Abilene, Kansas. The cattle were then sold at market and put on railroad cars and shipped east. During the peak months of the cattle season the population of a cow town could triple; for the town merchants it meant big business.

But cattle season was always a time for trouble, too. After a long drive most cowboys went "salooning," and it was common for a drunken cowboy to test his manhood by tangling with a sheriff. When a cowboy wanted to test his shooting skills on a sheriff, there wasn't much a lawman could do but shoot back. In the Old West a man who didn't know how to handle a gun didn't live long. That was especially true for the lawman.

The lawman—whether a sheriff or a marshal—was the true law on the frontier. A marshal patrolled the territories as a representative of the U.S. government, and a sheriff was hired to enforce laws passed by a town or county. Since courts were a luxury most towns couldn't afford, a lawman wielded enormous authority. A territorial judge might visit a town once or twice a year, but only for a few days. A dance hall or saloon would be converted into a temporary court, trials would be held, and judgments issued. Then the judge would pack up and head off to the next town. Often, however, a lawman became judge and jury. If a sheriff, for instance, felt he had good reason to arrest a man suspected of stealing a horse, he also had the authority to hang the man on the spot. It was fast justice. And there was never an appeal.

A lawman faced many dangers on the frontier. A posse tracking a gang of bandits, for instance, might travel for weeks through treacherous wilderness in terrible weather. If the bandits' bullets didn't kill a lawman on the trail, frostbite or starvation might. Summer heat could be just as deadly. There was always the risk, too, of ambush from Indians or attacks by bears, wolves, or snakes. For all the dangers a lawman faced on the frontier, he received no special training. His only qualifications were a quick draw, a cool temper, extraordinary courage, and a commitment to justice.

These six stories are but a few of the many that exist, and they form an unforgettable portrait of the men who helped tame the West.

TOM SMITH

Thomas James Smith was the son of Irish immigrants and a veteran of the New York City Police Department. Not much more than that is known about him until he arrived at Bear River, Wyoming, in 1867. The Union Pacific Railway was laying tracks into the mountains at the time, and the little towns that sprang up overnight along the railway were rough places indeed. At Bear River, Smith led a band of his fellow workers to save a boy wrongly accused of robbery from a mob of vigilantes. Badly beaten and shot several times, Smith so impressed the townsfolk with his bravery in defending the boy that Smith was named sheriff right then and there. After that he was known as "Bear River" Tom Smith. As the rails went west, so did Tom, cleaning up one little town after another. He moved south to Kit Carson, Colorado, in 1870. That's where he was when he heard that Abilene, Kansas, was looking for a new marshal.

The Man Who Tamed Abilene

Tom Smith reined in his gray mare at the top of a hill overlooking the town of Abilene. "Ho, Silverheels," he said. "Give me a few minutes to study the situation here."

He let his horse graze in the soft grass. It had been a long, hot ride from Kit Carson, Colorado, to Abilene, Kansas, and Silverheels was tired and slick with sweat.

Tom looked down across the rolling hills. The only sound was the rustling of the prairie grass in the wind. In the distance Abilene squatted on the prairie, surrounded by large herds of Texas longhorn cattle. Each year from May to September hundreds of thousands of cattle were driven up the Chisholm Trail from Texas to Abilene to be shipped east by rail. During those months Abilene was filled with rowdy Texas cowboys, every one of them trail weary and as wild as the wind.

Tom urged Silverheels into a trot. Word was out that Abilene needed a new marshal, and Tom wanted the job.

A big sign was posted at the edge of town: Warning! The Carrying of Firearms is Prohibited. Tom smiled. The sign was so riddled with bullet holes that he could barely make out the letters. He could even hear gunfire as he rode into town. It was July 4, 1870: Independence Day. Tom figured the cowboys must be celebrating.

Tom passed a small wooden structure with iron bars on the windows. A young deputy cringed inside the doorway as two drunken cowboys pranced around on their ponies and hurled insults at the jail.

"This calaboose is a danged Yankee insult I ain't goin' to tolerate!" one of the cowboys yelled. He fired his pistol into the air.

"And right here on Texas Street!" the other one cried. "It's an insult to Texas! We ought to bring along some boys and burn it down!" Both men fired a volley of shots into the sign above the door, then galloped off down the street laughing loudly and waving their guns in the air.

Tom calmly leaned over his saddle horn. "How come you didn't arrest them ol' boys for packin' guns in town?" he asked the deputy.

The deputy glowered. "And get myself killed?" he said. "Mayor McCoy only pays me to keep them Texans from pulling the roof off the calaboose again."

"Pretty rough town, you'd say?" asked Tom.

"Rough as they come, mister. We've done lost four marshals already, and Abilene's only three years old. The lawman who tames this town's gonna have to be a real bear."

"Well, my name's 'Bear River' Tom Smith," Tom laughed, "and I've been known to tame a town or two. Where do I go about finding your mayor?"

"Say, I've heard of you," said the deputy. "My name's

Johnny Jackson. You'll find Mayor McCoy's office out at the end of Railroad Street. You can't miss it. You can still read *his* sign." He gestured to the bullet-pocked sign above the jail door. "The mayor gets his sign repainted every week."

Tom tipped his hat in thanks and proceeded down Texas Street. Even at midday, cowboys staggered from one saloon to the next, every one of them armed to the teeth. All along the street, storefront windows were shot out, leaving jagged shards of glass around the window frames.

At the end of Railroad Street, Tom found the mayor's office nestled among some cottonwood trees. Half a dozen heavily armed men milled around the yard. They gathered menacingly around Tom as he dismounted.

"State your business, mister," one of them said to Tom.

"I'm Tom Smith. I've come to take the marshaling job here."

Just then the mayor, a little red-haired man with bristling eyebrows, came to the door. "Howdy. I'm Henry McCoy, mayor of Abilene." The two men shook hands.

"Well," McCoy said, "you sure look big enough to handle the job. But I've got to warn you that a lot of good men have tried to settle these cowpokes, without any luck. I just put the last marshal on a train back east—in a box."

"I was a policeman on the Bowery beat in New York City before I came west," Tom said, "and I've marshaled some of the railroad towns out in Wyoming. I haven't seen a lot of difference between the toughs in one place or the other. I know what I'm up against."

The mayor gave Tom a friendly slap on the back. "I believe you're the feller we've been looking for!" He fished around inside his pocket. "Here's the badge I took off the last marshal. Let's go do the swearing in."

That afternoon Marshal Smith began the hard business of taming Abilene. Unlike most frontier marshals, Tom didn't sling his guns in hip holsters. Instead, he kept a pair of small pistols in shoulder holsters, hidden from view beneath his coat. "This way," he explained to Johnny Jackson, "I ain't a walking dare for every cowpoke who wants to test out his fast draw on the new marshal."

Next, Tom hired workmen to put up new signs all over town banning firearms. From now on, Tom declared, anyone packing a firearm had to check in their pistols at their hotel or with a bartender before they could get a room or a drink. "Anybody foolish enough to make trouble," Tom proclaimed, "will have to answer to me."

The following evening, Tom and Johnny were helping the Crystal Palace saloonkeeper install a gun rack behind the bar when in walked trouble.

"His name is Big Hank," Johnny informed Tom. The scar-faced cowboy was packing a Colt .45 on each hip, and the handle of a huge bowie knife stuck out of one boot top.

Big Hank swaggered up to the bar. "I'll warrant you're the feller thinks he's gonna run this town," Hank sneered in Tom's direction.

Tom walked up to Big Hank. "I guess news don't grow much grass in Abilene," he said. "I'll trouble you to hand over your guns."

"Why don't you try and make me, mister?"

"Suit yourself," Tom said.

Tom swung, and landed a bone-crushing right hook

under Hank's jaw that lifted the cowboy clear off the floor. He crumpled into a heap at Tom's feet.

"Get his guns, Johnny, and that knife, too," said Tom. Turning his back on the flattened cowboy, Tom then asked the bartender if he could "oblige" him a cold drink. "Marshaling is thirsty business."

The news that Tom Smith had knocked Big Hank out with a single punch spread like prairie fire through the cow camps all around Abilene. Knocking out Big Hank earned Tom the grudging respect of the cowboys who knew him. And word quickly spread from one bunch of trail drivers to the next that the new marshal of Abilene was not to be tangled with. This spared Tom Smith a lot of grief.

Toward the end of August, however, a Texas cowboy named Jim Hatfield rode into town. He was tougher than ten-year-old saddle leather and as fast with a six-gun as a snake to a bite. In fact, the previous summer he had killed the Abilene marshal. He should have been hanged for the crime, but there wasn't a deputy within a hundred miles of Abilene foolish enough to arrest him. Thus, when Hatfield and his crew of twenty cowboys rode into Abilene that afternoon, he figured no man had the courage to stand up to him.

Hatfield and his cowboys immediately settled into the Old Fruit Saloon, but not before they ripped the gun racks off the wall and pitched them through the front window into the street. Deputy Johnny Jackson was in the Old Fruit at the time and he tried to stop them, but his luck was as bad as the gun racks'. Hatfield's boys flung him through the front window, too.

Tom found his deputy passed out cold in the dirt and carried him to the town's doctor.

"He'll be okay," said Doc, "but his head will be powerfully sore."

It was the evening of the next day before Johnny was fully awake. Tom tried to cheer him up with a gift—a brand-new silver-plated Colt Peacemaker.

"Much obliged," Johnny answered weakly.

Tom had one question. "Johnny, who pitched you through that window?"

"I'm sorry, Marshal," he mumbled groggily, "but I don't know exactly. It was a couple of new cowpokes. But it was Hatfield told them to do it."

"That's what I figured," Tom said. A few minutes later he was outside the Old Fruit Saloon. He shoved open the swinging doors and whistled low. Hatfield and his cowboys had managed to trash the saloon. Empty bottles littered the floor, chairs and tables were overturned, the mirror over the bar was shattered, and a few cowboys had fallen asleep in the corners.

One cowboy was leaning against the door as Tom came in. "Say, if it ain't the dadburned fistfightin' marshal! What's been keeping you? Visiting a sick deputy?" The cowboys standing around the saloon roared with laughter.

Tom backhanded the cowboy on the jaw. The man's head banged against the wall, and he fell facedown onto the floor. Suddenly a solid line of Hatfield's cowboys formed a tight half circle in front of Tom. Each one was packing a pistol.

Tom knew he couldn't outfight a saloon full of cowboys.

But he was as angry as a stirred-up den of rattlesnakes over what they had done to Johnny. He intended to make someone pay for it.

Tom Smith stared hard at the cowboys lined up in front of him. Some could hold his stare, some couldn't. Tom decided to break the tension with a bit of talk.

"I was in a situation like this one here once before," he said, "up in Bear River, Wyoming. I ended up taking six bullets. But four men died before I went down." As he spoke, his eyes wandered slowly from man to man. "Now, I'm just here to collar one man—Jim Hatfield. And I want each one of you cowpokes to think about this for a minute: Is this Hatfield feller worth dying for?"

The tiniest hint of a smile came to Tom's face as, slowly, one man after another began edging backward toward the walls. A space opened up in the middle of the room. There, in the center, stood Jim Hatfield, alone. His hands were hovering above a pair of well-worn pistols.

"I got to give you this much, Smith," Hatfield said. "You're pretty good at speechifying. But I ain't heard nothing about your gunplay. I think you're gonna have to do some shooting to get yourself out of here."

Tom took two steps forward, closing the gap between himself and Hatfield. "Well," Tom said, "I reckon you must have decided today is your day to die."

Hatfield's draw was like a flash of lightning. Just as quickly, Tom leaped forward and slapped the gun out of Hatfield's right hand. At the same time he yanked Hatfield's second gun out of its holster and pitched it over the bar. Hatfield swung at Tom and connected with a solid punch in

the ribs. Tom staggered, and Hatfield whipped out a foot-long bowie knife.

"I'm gonna leave you in pieces all over this floor," he snarled, dropping into a crouch. He began to circle Tom. Suddenly he lunged forward, slashing with the big blade. Tom caught Hatfield's wrist with his right hand. With his left he grabbed Hatfield by the throat and lifted him off the floor.

Hatfield sputtered and gasped. "I think you're done with cutting up folks for a while," Tom told him. He slapped the hand that held the knife against the bar, sending the blade skittering across the floor.

Tom was pleased to see two of his deputies, the mayor, and a crowd of citizens at the door. The deputies stepped into the saloon with their guns drawn.

"I'm taking this miserable excuse of a human being to the calaboose," Tom said. "And I expect the mayor will want you cowboys to make a good-size donation to help fix this place up."

"That's for dang sure," said Mayor McCoy. "I want every one of you to empty your pockets on this table. From the looks of it, you boys have a whole saloon to pay for."

"You can start by dropping them gun belts," Tom said as he hauled Hatfield to the door. To Tom's ears the thudding sound of twenty gun belts hitting the floor was very satisfying.

"Ain't he something?" said the mayor proudly as Tom left. "He's half cougar and half coiled snake. And he's a particular friend of mine."

WILLIE KENNARD

There were very few black sheriffs on the frontier, though there were many black scouts, two regiments of black cavalry troopers, and a few former slaves who had escaped their masters and joined various Indian bands.   Willie Kennard was a former slave who joined the Ninth Cavalry Regiment, U.S. Army, shortly after the Civil War.   He served with distinction and then moved west, where he became the sheriff of the mining town of Yankee Hill, Colorado.   This is his story.

Ex-Slave and Buffalo Soldier

Sergeant Willie Kennard felt no sadness when he left Fort Richardson for the last time. Instead, he felt like a king. For the first time in his life, he realized, he was truly free. Born a slave, he had signed on as a soldier with the Ninth U.S. Cavalry immediately after the Civil War. It was a good life—exciting, with generally good food and fairly decent pay—yet Willie realized now that he had never been totally on his own. There had always been someone to tell him what to do and when to do it, whether it was his old master or some officer. This was a big step.

Willie rode slowly past his former platoon, acknowledging each trooper with a nod or a cheerful wink. The men saluted him. He rode past the new lieutenant, fresh from West Point, without even glancing at him. He rode past the guards at the gate and out onto the north Texas prairie, where he stopped and turned for one last look at the fort.

"That's a sorry-looking place to call home," he muttered. He stood up in his stirrups, took off his hat, and waved it in a wild circle. "Yeeee-ha!" he yelled. He was as happy as a mockingbird.

Willie rode west for two weeks, and each new sunrise made him realize what a wonderful thing it was to be his own master. He was proud to have been a soldier, especially a member of the first all-black cavalry regiment. He had also been one of the few black sergeants in the whole U.S. Army. For seven years he had fought Comanche, Kiowa, and even Sioux all over Kansas and Nebraska. He had wanted his sergeant's stripes more than anything in the world. And he had earned them the hard way.

Now he had a dream. Willie wanted to be a lawman. He wanted to wear a silver star and be called "Mr. Sheriff, sir." That's why he was headed west toward the wild mining country of Colorado. He had been told that there were hundreds of little towns there in desperate need of lawmen.

After crossing the Wichita and Pease rivers, Willie followed the Prairie Dog Fork of the Red River until he found himself in the middle of Palo Duro Canyon, near Amarillo. Making his way up onto the northern rim of the canyon, Willie came upon a crew of buffalo hunters.

"Y'all need yourselves another rifle?" he asked one of the hunters.

"We might could use the rifle," sneered a hunter. "But ain't no black finger gonna be on the trigger," warned another. "If you want a job, boy, you get on down there with the skinners," he said, pointing east. "They're out there about a mile or so."

Willie shook his head and nudged his horse in the direction indicated. At the crest of a small hill, Willie looked down and saw hundreds of buffalo carcasses littering the

plains. Crews of greasy, foul-smelling men worked their way from one carcass to the next, followed by clouds of flies.

"Willie Kennard," he told himself disgustedly, "there are places in hell that smell sweeter than this. You'd best just keep on moving."

One month after leaving Fort Richardson, Willie Kennard hitched his pony in front of a little café in the town of Raton, just below the pass in the Rocky Mountains that would take him into the high Colorado country.

Living on fish and game had suited Willie just fine, but it was good to finally sit at a table and drink hot, sweet coffee from a clean cup and be served beefsteak and fried eggs and some curious flat bread called tortillas.

He finished off his meal by studying the Help Wanted section of a week-old copy of the *Rocky Mountain News*. Liverymen were needed. So were miners, cooks, piano players, and bartenders. Then he saw the Lawmen Wanted section and found several advertisements for sheriffs in little mining towns all over the Colorado Rockies.

"Well now," Willie said to himself, "there's only three things a lawman needs to be: brave, levelheaded, and good with a gun, and I do seem to fit that bill."

The next day Willie headed north across Raton Pass to Cripple Creek, Colorado, one of the little towns looking for a sheriff. But when he rode into Cripple Creek, he learned that a new sheriff had already been hired.

"Look," said Sheriff Jonas Wylie when he heard of Willie's plans, "I know what you buffalo soldiers were up against out in Kansas. I know that you'd probably make as good a lawman as any. Probably better than most."

Willie smiled. Indians called the black cavalry "buffalo soldiers" because in battle they had proved themselves to be as tough as the big animals. Being called a buffalo by an Indian was a compliment.

"Well, Sheriff," admitted Willie, "I ain't no Bill Hickok, but I've done some fighting all right."

"It ain't that." The sheriff shook his head sadly. "To tell the truth, friend, you're gonna have to look into some pretty desperate situations before you find a town full of white men willing to hire a black sheriff. That's the sorry truth of it. But I wish you luck."

Wylie was right. Folks in town after town made it clear that as a black man, Willie Kennard was unwelcome. But Willie refused to quit. He had come too far to give up. He was going to be a lawman. So Willie rode on, higher and higher into the mountains, over Red Hill Pass and Kenosha Pass, and finally around Mount Bierstadt and over Guenella Pass, where there was snow on the ground even in midsummer.

Finally, one evening just at sunset, he came to Yankee Hill, a ramshackle mining town huddled on the top of a windblown hill.

On the outskirts of town, Willie considered making camp in a small grove of white-skinned aspen trees. It was a peaceful spot, and Willie was looking forward to a warm cup of coffee and a long snooze before heading in to see the mayor about a job. But off in the distance he suddenly heard some shouting, then a couple of gunshots. Willie decided to put off the coffee. "This might be just the right time to take a look at the town," he told himself.

Yankee Hill was a one-street town, with only a half-dozen or so buildings on either side. All were dark except one: Gaylor's Saloon. Willie peered in through one of its dirty windows and whistled low. Gaylor's was a far cry from the glittering saloons of Abilene, with their chandeliers and roulette wheels and pretty serving girls. Here there were smoky lanterns, one long bar, and a few plank tables. "Ain't much to speak of, is it?" Willie mumbled to himself.

Just then a man came flying through the double swinging doors and crashed headlong into the street, groaning. The man looked to be less than five feet tall and was thin as a rail. But Willie was even more surprised when a man as big as a bear burst through the doors and charged after him. The little man cowered as the big man hovered over him, both .45s drawn. "Get up, you lousy mosquito!" the big man roared. The little man rolled over, and Willie could see the flash of a silver star. It was the sheriff.

"Please, Mr. Casewit," the sheriff whimpered. "Don't go and do nothing you'll regret later on. I just came down here to ask you boys to keep it down a bit so's the citizens round about here can get some sleep. I ain't out to arrest nobody or anything!"

"Get out of the dust, bub," growled the big man. "I done whipped one sheriff already, and you ain't half the man he was." The big man suddenly grinned. "On the other hand, you're such a tiny little runt, I bet you'd make better target shooting than a Texas jackrabbit. I'll tell you what: I'll count to ten before I start shooting. I suggest that you high-tail it out of *my* town lickety-split. One! Two!"

Willie loosened his gun in his holster. He wasn't about

to let a man get shot in the back. But by the time the big man had counted to ten, there was no trace of the sheriff. The big man laughed and stomped back into the saloon.

"Well, well," thought Willie. "I reckon this town's done lost a sheriff today. I might just luck into the job tomorrow." Later, after making camp, Willie stretched out in his bedroll and watched the stars twinkling through the aspen leaves above him. "Yes sir, Mr. Kennard," he said to himself, "tomorrow may be your lucky day."

The next morning Willie stopped at a small café called Fat Sarah's Eatery. He ordered a fried steak and a bowl of beans. At another table a thin man in a shabby black coat was talking to a large man with a gold watch chain draped across his vest.

"Lookee here, Mayor," said the thin man. "I've already buried a U.S. marshal and three sheriffs so far this year. As undertaker in this town, ain't I supposed to get paid when I bury a public servant?"

"You'll get paid," said the mayor impatiently. "Right now I got more important matters to consider, like finding me a man fool enough to become our new sheriff!"

" 'Scuse me," Willie said, walking up to the table. "Am I right that you're in need of a sheriff in this here town?"

The mayor eyed him suspiciously. "That's right. My last one run off just yesterday. What's it to you, boy?"

Willie bristled at the slur. He was nearly forty years old and stood a full foot taller than the mayor. "I'm your man, Mr. Mayor," he said. "The name's Willie Kennard, formerly a sergeant of the Ninth U.S. Cavalry. I want to be your sheriff."

The mayor and the undertaker exchanged bewildered glances, then burst out laughing. "You do, do you?" the mayor said. "Get on with you, boy. We got a gunslinger in this town who'd shoot off all ten of your fingers before you could slap leather on him. Fact is," the mayor added ruefully, "he's made a danged profession out of shooting sheriffs and marshals."

"Well," Willie said, "settling gunslingers is what sheriffs is for, ain't they? You put that star on me and I'll go and bring in your gunslinger for you."

The undertaker snorted. "Heck, Mayor, if he wants to die that bad, why don't you oblige him?" He looked Willie up and down. "But tall as he is, the coffin's going to cost you a dollar extra."

"Tell you what, Mr. Mayor," Willie said, "I got twenty-three dollars in the saddlebags on my pony out there. If you have to bury me, you can use the money to pay this old gravedigger here."

The mayor nodded his head slowly. "I think you mean what you say, boy. There's just one thing. I want you to bring back that sheriff-shooting son of a gun alive."

Willie nodded in agreement. "This here outlaw got a name?" he asked.

"Barney Casewit," said the mayor.

Willie said, "I figured that was who you meant. I saw him run your last sheriff out of town last night."

"Then you know that you're up against as ornery an old coot as ever set foot in the mountains. You bring me Casewit in one piece and you can wear that badge as long as you want.

I want the pleasure of stringing him up on Main Street myself."

"Done," said Willie, putting out his hand to shake on it. "But I got one thing to add to the bargain."

"What's that?" asked the mayor.

"If I do what I say I will, you promise you won't ever call me 'boy' again."

The mayor nodded. "Fair enough by me," he said. The mayor pinned the star on Willie's jacket. Willie noticed that it had only four points.

"The other point done got shot off," the mayor explained. "I'll send for a new star if you come back wearing that one." He pointed down the street. "You'll find Casewit and some of his outlaw friends down at Gaylor's Saloon."

"I know where it is," said Willie.

"Well then," the mayor chuckled, "good luck."

Willie turned to go, but the undertaker stopped him. "How tall *are* you?" he asked.

"Don't you be worrying about that right now," Willie answered.

The undertaker shrugged. "Suit yourself."

Willie checked the chambers of his Colt revolver as he walked down the short street, then holstered it lightly. He paused in front of Gaylor's and drew his breath, slow and even. Next, he loosened some cartridges in his belt just in case he had to reload.

"Barney Casewit!" he hollered. "You're wanted by the law for killin' too many men to name! I'm the law here now, and I want you out here with your hands up!"

The raucous laughter inside the saloon suddenly hushed.

"Hey, Barn!" someone shouted. "Get a load of what the mayor sent down this time!"

Barney Casewit shoved open the saloon doors and let them slap together behind him. "You're the new sheriff?" he snarled. "I think our mayor is down to the bottom of the barrel! What do you think, boys?"

There was laughter from inside the saloon, and the sound of chairs raking across the floor. Willie saw several grinning faces appear at the windows on either side of the door. Casewit wore a six-gun on each hip, but Willie noticed that he favored his right hand. He would have to hit his right hand first, Willie reasoned, then the left. After all, he wanted to bring Casewit back alive.

"Mayor says he wants to hang you," Willie said, smiling politely. "So I ain't supposed to kill you. Just bring you in."

"I'll give you this much," Casewit said. "You got a lot of grit to come down here wearing the same tin star I already done put a hole through."

"Well, let's just see if I get to keep it."

Casewit's hands flicked backward for his two revolvers.

But Willie had him beat. His pistol bucked as he fired. The black revolver in Casewit's right hand jerked and spun away as Casewit took a bullet through his hand.

Casewit fired with his left hand, but the shot carried wide to Willie's left. Willie fired a second shot, wounding Casewit in the left arm. The big man dropped his gun and fell to his knees, helplessly clutching his wounded hand and arm.

Willie heard the shattering of glass, and several of Casewit's men began firing wildly into the street. Willie jumped sideways, dropped to the ground, and rolled once as a haze of bullets peppered the dirt. He fired into one window, rolled again, and fired into the other. Suddenly the shooting from inside the saloon stopped. Willie stood slowly, covering every inch of the saloon with his eyes. He had only two bullets left in his gun. If there was to be any more shooting, he would have no time to reload. But there was no more shooting. Willie calmly walked over to Casewit, who was still on his knees.

Willie put the barrel of his revolver to Casewit's temple and yanked him up off the ground by his collar. "Barney Casewit," he said, "you're under arrest. Let's go down to the calaboose."

What had been the deserted main street of Yankee Hill was now filled with cheering miners, their wives, and their children. "Some shooting!" he heard them say. "Did you see it?" they asked each other. The townsfolk lined a path down the street for Willie and his prisoner. In front of Fat Sarah's, the mayor joined the parade. He led the way to a tiny shack at the edge of town.

The mayor handed the jail keys to Willie. "Sheriff," he said, "lock up your prisoner."

After Willie had locked Casewit away in the calaboose, the mayor turned to address the crowd. "Citizens of Yankee Hill," he intoned, "let me introduce you to *Mister* Willie Kennard, former buffalo soldier, and our new sheriff."

WYATT EARP

U.S. Army surveyors warned prospector Ed Schieffelin that all he would find at the barren southern end of Arizona's San Pedro valley would be his tombstone. That's why, when Schieffelin discovered silver there in 1877, he named the place Tombstone.

Soon prospectors swarmed into the arid hills. Tombstone, Arizona, grew from one person to fifteen thousand people within two years. It became known as the most lawless city on earth, ruled by gangs of rustlers and bandits.

U.S. marshal Wyatt Earp had tamed Dodge City, the wildest of the Kansas cow towns, and was ready to move on. When the citizens of Tombstone began to cry out for law and order, Wyatt answered that call. With his brothers Virgil and Morgan, and his good friend Doc Holliday, as his deputies, Wyatt Earp took over as the sheriff of Pima County, Arizona, on December 1, 1879. Shortly afterward he became U.S. marshal. The first order of business was to clean up the Clanton and McLowerey gangs.

Showdown at the O.K. Corral

Being a lawman in Tombstone meant keeping late hours. Allen Street and Fremont Street, the town's two wide dirt thoroughfares, were lined with saloons—the Oriental Saloon and Gambling Hall, the Crystal Palace, the Alhambra, and a dozen others—all of which stayed open until nearly dawn. Anything could happen, and generally did. Most nights Wyatt Earp and his deputies were kept busy rounding up rowdy miners and gunslinging gamblers, then hauling them off to the calaboose. That's why Wyatt was eating breakfast at noon when a local rancher named Fred Daly came looking for him.

Daly sat down opposite Wyatt and took off his huge sombrero. "Marshal," he said, "I got to warn you. Ike Clanton is making noises like he means to bushwhack you."

"I'm not surprised," said Wyatt, as calm as if Daly had just told him that the sun was hot in Arizona. "A while back I put his best friend, Frank Stillwell, in jail over in Tucson for robbing the Tombstone-Bisbee stagecoach. He's been promising to get his revenge ever since."

"I just thought I ought to warn you," Daly said.

"You have my thanks, Mr. Daly," Wyatt said. He rose from the table and put on his black Stetson. "I don't doubt that Ike would shoot me in the back if he had the chance, but he'll have to get round to that side of me first."

Ike Clanton and his four brothers were former cattle rustlers who had recently switched to robbing stages. There were forty to fifty renegade cowboys in their gang, and each one was just as wild and wicked as Ike.

Walking down Allen Street toward his office, Wyatt grinned at the thought of Frank Stillwell. He and a partner had stolen a twenty-five-thousand-dollar payroll locked in a Wells-Fargo strongbox. Their biggest mistake, however, at least as far as Wyatt was concerned, was that they also had stolen the U.S. Mail sack. *That* made the robbery a federal offense and U.S. marshal Wyatt Earp's business.

Wyatt took it as part of his job to observe potential lawbreakers very closely. A marshal never knew when he might have to identify some outlaw by his hat or his horse or his boots. One day in the Alhambra Saloon about a month before the robbery, Wyatt had passed by Stillwell, who was leaning back in a chair, feet up on the table. Wyatt noticed a curious pattern of crossed nailheads on the heel of Stillwell's boot.

Later, when Wyatt began to investigate the site of the stage robbery, he immediately recognized a similar pattern of bootheel tracks in the dirt. All Wyatt had to do was go back to Tombstone and arrest Frank Stillwell . . . and his boots. It was one of the easiest arrests in Wyatt's experience. He found both the money and the mail in Stillwell's hotel room.

Stillwell's arrest had cost the Clantons a lot of money. It was no surprise, then, that Ike was hot for revenge.

Wyatt loosened his Buntline Special in its holster. The .45 Colt revolver, with its extra-long barrel, was his trademark gun. As far as Wyatt could tell, the length of the barrel hadn't slowed down his draw any, and he appreciated the gun's superior accuracy. On his left hip, slung a little higher than the Buntline, Wyatt carried a plain .45 Peacemaker.

Wyatt flexed his fingers and popped his knuckles. That was all the preparation he ever made for a gunfight. He walked down Allen Street and crossed onto Fremont. He decided he would round up his brothers and let them know that the Clantons were looking for trouble.

On Fremont Street a barmaid named Millie Baker pulled Wyatt aside. "Mr. Earp," she said, "there was some trouble last night at the Occidental you ought to know about. Ike Clanton and Doc Holliday got into a scrape, and your brother Morgan had to pull Doc out of it before there was a shootout."

"Thank you, Millie. I heard a little about it already this morning."

"Well," Millie said, "Ike sure was on a tear." She took the marshal's arm in hers as they walked. Millie had a warm spot for the handsome young marshal.

"Ike got all worked up and swore that he was going to gun down you and Doc," she said. "So you be careful, you hear?"

"I will," said Wyatt, smiling. "Now you'd best run along, Millie." He was still grinning to himself when he rounded a corner and ran smack into Ike Clanton.

"Well, if it ain't our good marshal himself," Ike snarled. "You tell that Doc Holliday that no man can talk to me the way he did and live. I wasn't wearing a gun last night, but I am now. You tell that no-account friend of yours he better say himself some prayers, 'cause I mean to get him."

"Doc's still in bed, and you're still half drunk," Wyatt said. "But you better not tangle with him. He'll cut down a slow-handed snake like you before you get your gun cocked."

"I ain't afraid of you," Ike said as he mounted his pony. "I'm coming to town tomorrow to clean you Earps out of Tombstone," Clanton growled. "And I'm bringing friends. You remember, Earp. Tomorrow!"

"It'll be me doing the cleaning, Ike. And it'll be you and your skunk brothers that will go out with the trash."

Cursing all the Earps ever born, Ike yanked on the reins, spurred his horse, and galloped down the street.

Wyatt was awakened early the next morning by his brothers Virgil and Morgan banging on his door.

"Ike wasn't fooling around," Virgil told Wyatt. "He and his brothers and Tom and Frank McLowerey are all down at Fifth and Allen streets, armed to the teeth. They're saying that they mean to drive out all us Earps."

"I should have known he'd rustle up those McLowerey snakes," Wyatt said.

The McLowerey brothers had plenty of reason to hate Wyatt Earp. Until Wyatt had arrived in Tombstone, the McLowereys had made a good living robbing stages of silver bullion shipments and payrolls. But Wyatt had put an end to that, and recently they had been reduced to rustling cattle. It was common knowledge around Tombstone that the Mc-

Lowereys would like nothing better than to see Wyatt Earp take up new lodgings—preferably six feet under.

Wyatt made some hasty plans. "Morgan, you and Virgil go up Fremont Street. I'll take Allen Street. No doubt that yellowbelly will have sobered up some, and you'll probably find him crouched down somewhere, waiting to bushwhack us. If you see him, go ahead and arrest him."

Sure enough, Morgan and Virgil spotted Clanton hiding in the shadows in an alley looking out onto Allen Street. He was peering down the long barrel of a Winchester. Very quietly, the two brothers crept up behind him.

"Are you waiting for someone, you snake-eyed skunk?" Virgil whispered.

Ike was so surprised, he jumped like a startled cat. He whirled and tried to bring his Winchester around, but Virgil hurled himself against the barrel, pressing it against the wall. With his right hand he jerked his Colt and brought it down with a *thunk* on Clanton's skull. Ike collapsed like a sack of flour. The brothers dragged him out of the alley and up the street to the little Tombstone jail.

Trials were often quick affairs in Tombstone, and it was only an hour later that Ike Clanton was standing in front of the judge. He was fined twenty-five dollars for disturbing the peace and was ordered to leave town. Clanton left the court muttering threats at the Earps.

"That fine ain't going to do much but rile him up even more," Virgil told Wyatt.

"Don't worry," Wyatt told him. "We'll be ready for him, whatever he does."

For the rest of the day the streets were empty, except every now and then when small groups of the Clanton and McLowerey gangs staggered into or out of a saloon. In every window, however, there were anxious faces. Everyone knew that the simmering feud between the Earps and the Clantons was about to come to a boil.

Late that afternoon a man named Horace Pettigrew burst into the marshal's office. "Wyatt!" he called out. "There's trouble brewing down at my corral."

Wyatt stared calmly at Pettigrew from behind his desk. Morgan Earp was in a chair to the side. "What seems to be the problem, Horace?" Wyatt asked.

"Ike Clanton and his crowd have been drinking all day, and they're getting hot. They're making gun-talk against you fellers. They're hiding out near my corral. I guess they figure to ambush you." He shook his head. "I wouldn't set foot in the street if I was an Earp for all the silver in Tombstone."

"Well, you ain't an Earp," Wyatt pointed out.

"Thank goodness for that," Pettigrew said. He nodded at Virgil Earp as he came in, then turned back to Wyatt. "What are y'all going to do about it, Marshal? I can't get no livery business done with that crowd down there."

"I guess they've got to have their lesson," said Wyatt, turning to his brothers. "Reckon we'd better go down to the corral and surprise them before they surprise us."

Just then another of Wyatt's deputies, R. J. Coleman, came in with a message from Frank McLowerey. "He says come on down to the corral and fight it out now, or they'll come burn down the office here and pick you off one at a time if you try to get out."

"That's it," said Wyatt. "Let's go, boys."

Walking three abreast, Wyatt, Virgil, and Morgan Earp were halfway down Fourth Street when they met Doc Holliday.

"Where are you going, Wyatt?" he called out.

"Down the street to answer an insult," replied Wyatt. "But this one's ours, Doc. There's no need for you to mix in."

"That's a heck of a thing to say to your best friend," said Doc. "I've been hearing about this Ike Clanton ruckus all day. I didn't figure that you'd go without me!"

"That's awfully friendly of you, Doc," Wyatt said, pausing for a moment. "This'll be a tough one."

"Tough ones are the kind I like best."

"All right then, Doc," said Wyatt.

The four men walked side by side as they turned onto Fremont Street and passed the Papago Cash Store and Bauer's market. At the end of the street, just past Fly's Photographic Gallery, was Horace Pettigrew's O.K. Corral.

Ike Clanton, his brother Billy, Tom and Frank Mc-Lowerey, and a rustler named William Claiborne walked slowly out of the O.K. Corral and into an empty lot adjacent to the gallery. Their hands danced nervously at their sides.

Wyatt and his men took up positions in the lot with their backs to the gallery. Only twenty feet separated one group from the other.

"You skunks are under arrest," said Wyatt. "Throw up your hands."

Frank McLowerey laughed. "There ain't none of you buzzards that's got the grit to stand and fight," he shouted. "Why don't you skedaddle on back to Kansas?"

"Well, Frank," said Virgil modestly, "Wyatt's done plumb run out of low-down skunks in Kansas, so we had to come out here looking for more." He smiled. "I'd say we hit the jackpot," Virgil said. "Skunkwise, that is."

"Stop your yammering," Ike snarled. "Are you gonna draw—or *talk* us to death?"

Wyatt kept his eyes bolted to Ike Clanton's hands. When talking to a man there was always a temptation to look him in the eye. But Wyatt always watched the man's hands. Wyatt smiled. Ike's fingers twitched fretfully over his holster.

"You can put your hands up, Ike," Wyatt said, "or you can get to fighting. It's the same to me, either way."

Ike shot a nervous glance at Billy. Suddenly Frank and Billy simultaneously jerked their guns and fired. The explosion was like thunder. Bullets tore through Wyatt's coat sleeves as he drew his gun matter-of-factly and returned fire. Frank went down like a load of bricks. Morgan went down, too, wounded in the shoulder. Billy squeezed off two shots before he, too, fell facedown into the dirt.

Ike suddenly panicked and ran like a scared rabbit out the back of the lot. William Claiborne fired twice at Virgil, missed both times, and ran for cover into the open door of the photographic gallery.

In the confusion of gunfire and smoke, Tom McLowerey managed to escape into the street. Doc ran after him. "Hold it right there or I'll fire!" yelled Doc. But McLowerey kept running until a single shot from Doc's silver-plated Colt brought him down.

At the same time the side window of Fly's Photographic Gallery shattered, and William Claiborne opened fire, raising dust just inches from where Morgan was still lying on the ground.

"Look out!" shouted Wyatt. He spun and put four quick shots into the open window. Wyatt heard a muffled cry and the thump of William Claiborne collapsing to the floor. Wyatt calmly returned his revolver to his holster.

Doc walked over just as Wyatt was helping Morgan to his feet. "Ike got away," he told Wyatt.

"I reckon he couldn't have gotten far," the marshal replied quietly.

"I wish I could have cut him down," Morgan said.

"He'll get what's due him," Wyatt said. "I'll see to that."

Ike Clanton was arrested later the same day. The gunfight at the O.K. Corral—the most famous gunfight in the old West—was over in less than a minute.

BAT MASTERSON

Canadian by birth, William Barclay "Bat" Masterson moved with his family in 1865 to a farm in southern Illinois.   In 1872, at the age of nineteen, Bat convinced two of his four brothers that farm life was too dull, and they set out to find their fortune in the West.   After a short stint of hard work with the Santa Fe Railway, Bat became a buffalo hunter.   He also worked as a scout and a teamster and finally became sheriff of Ford County, Kansas.

The Capture of the Rudabaugh Gang

"Sheriff!" boomed a voice from the open door of the Western Union telegraph office. Bat Masterson stopped on the street and turned. The telegraph operator called, "Better get over here!"

The door slammed shut quickly against the blowing snow that swirled down the main street of Dodge City. Bat Masterson hurried across the street, leaning heavily on his silver-headed ebony cane. The cane had come in handy once when Bat was recovering from a gunshot wound in the leg. Now it more often served as a weapon than as a crutch. The bitterly cold weather, however, had made the old wound ache, and Bat's limp was worse than usual.

As Bat clomped up the stairs, the door to the telegraph office was thrown open by Charlie Bassett, one of Bat's deputies. "Dave Rudabaugh's gang is on the loose again," he said as Bat walked in. Charlie handed Bat a telegraph message.

Bassett, the telegraph operator, and some other men made room for Bat to warm his backside at the potbellied wood stove.

"Well," Bat said, folding up the telegram, "you have to

hand it to the Rudabaugh gang for choosing the right time of year to rob a train." He explained to the men that according to the message from the sheriff in Edwards County, Rudabaugh's gang had robbed the Santa Fe Express two nights before near Kinsley, about forty miles northeast of Dodge City. The train had been pushing slowly through a snowdrift when the gang boarded. They hadn't even had to block the tracks. Bat shook his head. "He might as well have had tickets!"

The Edwards County sheriff had sent a posse out after the gang, but they needed help.

"Rustle up a posse, Charlie," Bat said.

Charlie nodded. "You'll need some good trackers in this snow."

"Yes," said Bat. "But I need some fellers with grit as well. Rudabaugh's a huge son of a gun and as mean as they come. Get me Josh Webb and Big Kinch Riley."

Just then the telegraph began rattling with another message.

"It's from the sheriff in Edwards County again," the operator said, sitting down to copy out the message letter by letter. He read it out loud as it came in: "Gang crossed Arkansas River and turned south. Stop. Trail's gone cold. Stop. Headed for the sandhill country. Stop. Good luck. Stop." He turned to look at Bat. "End of message."

"The sandhill country is just south of here," said Bat. "I did some buffalo hunting there a few years back. We'd best get going or we'll lose him for sure. If we don't catch up to him in a couple of days, he'll make a break for the Indian territory. He knows we'd never go after him down there if it meant we might have to fight Indians, too."

The next morning at dawn, Bat swore in his posse. Big Kinch Riley was a burly redhead who stood six-foot-two. Bat knew his large fists would come in handy if they had to take on Rudabaugh man to man.

Josh Webb worked as a cook at the Long Ranch Saloon. He was half Cherokee and one of the best trackers Bat had ever known.

Heading out of Dodge City, the three men forded the half-frozen Arkansas River and continued south, pushed along by a fierce wind that lashed their backs with sleet. By midday the sky was the color of gunmetal. As the posse trudged across the flat, trackless landscape, Bat knew it was only a matter of time before the snow would begin to fall in earnest. And that would only make the job of tracking Rudabaugh that much more difficult. The men rode hunched over in their saddles with their hats pulled down over their eyes. Just as they reached Crooked Creek, twenty-seven long miles from Dodge City, the snow began to fall.

"Better find a place to bed down, Bat," Big Kinch called out. "Rudabaugh's tough, but he ain't tougher than this storm!"

Bat nodded in agreement and pointed ahead to a small grove of cottonwood trees. Josh and Kinch gathered firewood while Bat saw to the horses. For shelter, Bat rigged a lean-to out of a blanket to act as a windbreak. A pile of thick brush was dragged up to form a second wall. Soon all three men were huddled around a tiny fire waiting for a panful of snow to melt down to water. When the water boiled, Josh poured in a stiff measure of ground coffee.

"Here you go, gents," Josh said, pouring the steaming

coffee into their waiting tin cups. "I'll bet this is as good as anything I could brew at the Long Branch back in Dodge."

"Maybe," said Bat, laughing, "except you're a poor substitute for Miss Eliza." Eliza Warren was everyone's favorite waitress at the Long Branch Saloon.

"It's true enough about Eliza," said Big Kinch, puffing contentedly on his pipe, "but Josh is sure right about the coffee. I can't remember a time when coffee tasted any better."

Next, Josh fried up some potatoes and beef jerky for supper. The men ate greedily, not knowing exactly when they might have another hot meal.

All that night hungry wolves howled in the darkness just beyond the camp, causing the horses to fidget and stamp nervously. To protect the horses, Bat instructed each man to keep a three-hour watch while the other two slept. Bat cautioned them not to shoot at the wolves unless they actually attacked the horses. "Rudabaugh and his gang could be close by without our knowing it," Bat explained. "And a rifle shot would be an engraved invitation about where we are."

The next morning at dawn the posse broke camp quickly. "If we want to catch up with Rudabaugh," Bat told his deputies, "we'll have to keep moving." So instead of a nice breakfast of bacon and eggs and hot coffee, they chewed on cold beef jerky. They rode for hours through deep drifts of fresh snow until, around midday, they came to the top of a hill from which they could see for miles in all directions, but nothing moved in all that silent, frozen landscape.

"If Rudabaugh was out there somewhere," Josh said, "we'd have seen him. The man's as big as a buffalo."

"That ought to make him easy to track," laughed Kinch, "but I sure don't see anything moving."

Bat chose another hill to the south as a landmark and led the posse in its direction, picking his way slowly through the two-foot-deep layer of snow. Speed was essential, but so was caution. Drifts of snow could hide sudden drop-offs, and a horse could easily be lamed by stepping on a sharp rock or into a prairie-dog hole hidden beneath the snow.

Bat and his companions reached the summit of the second hill late that afternoon. But Rudabaugh and his gang were still nowhere to be seen.

"It looks like we ain't having no luck at all," Bat said. He peered up into the darkening sky. "Night's coming on," he said. "We'd best make camp."

The mood around the camp was gloomy. It seemed colder than the night before, and there were no trees to provide shelter from the wind.

"At least we know there ain't nobody within hearing distance if we need to shoot a wolf," Big Kinch said. His pipe glowed in the dusk, and he cupped his hands around it for warmth as he surveyed the hillside. He shivered, and pulled his coat tight around him. "I reckon this is like to be a pretty cold camp, fellers," he said. "I wish we'd had sense to pack along some firewood."

"Well, I'm going to get some sleep anyway," Bat told him. "Cover me up with snow once I'm rolled up in my blanket. You can take the first watch."

Kinch covered both Josh and Bat with a thick insulating layer of snow, and the two men slept. But it was a bone-weary sleep, and both men felt nearly frozen. Except for the mournful howling of the wind, there wasn't a sound that could be heard all night. Even the wolves were huddled silently in their dens. The only sound that broke the silence was the grumbling of first Bat and then Josh when the time came for each to take his watch.

The next morning the three men were cold, stiff, and groggy. Bat noticed that Josh appeared particularly sickly. "Seems to me, Sheriff," Josh said, hiding a cough with his fist, "that we'd better find some place to warm up or we're gonna end up dead. Besides, we haven't struck anybody's trail so far."

"Rudabaugh's probably thinking the same thing about now," Bat said. He slapped his thighs and stamped his feet to warm himself. "There's only one place I can think of to go, and I'll bet good money that Rudabaugh knows about it, too."

"You thinking of old Harry Lovell's place?" asked Kinch.

"That's right. We should be about ten miles from it now, due west. Let's hope we get there before Rudabaugh does. I'd sure like to thaw out some before I have to do any shooting." He looked from Kinch to Josh, then back to Kinch. "It looks like Josh here is coming down sick on us."

Josh straightened up from another coughing fit. "I'll make it," he said. "But I wouldn't turn down anybody's campfire right now."

The ride to Lovell's ranch was hard going and slow. The sun came out around noon, but it was a harsh, blinding light that reflected off the snow and burned their eyes. By the time dusk fell, all three men were having trouble seeing.

Still, they plodded on slowly, mile after frozen mile. Fortunately the moon shone brightly in the cloudless sky, allowing them enough light to find their way. Finally, at around ten o'clock, Josh picked up the scent of woodsmoke on the wind.

"Can't smell it myself," said Kinch, sniffing loudly.

"You've been breathing that rotten pipe smoke so long it's a wonder you can smell anything," said Bat. "But I trust Josh's nose."

After a while the men came upon a clearing where a crooked chimney poked out from a small snow-covered cabin.

"You sure the smoke you smelled came from Lovell's chimney?" Big Kinch whispered to Josh. "His place is buried clear up to the gills in snow. You reckon he's even here?"

They dismounted, and Bat told them to wait in the clearing while he checked the barn for signs of Rudabaugh. Inside, there was dry hay and water, two horses, and five cows.

"Lovell's here," Bat said, coming out of the barn. "The ice on the water trough's been broken recently. But I don't see any extra horses in here that might be Rudabaugh's. Come on, boys; let's get indoors."

Just then there was a clatter as Josh and his saddle collapsed in a heap. "Dang," Bat said. "Kinch, help me carry Josh inside."

"Heck," said Kinch, easily lifting Josh in his arms, "his blanket weighs more than he does! You'd think a cook would have more fat on his bones."

"Lovell!" Bat shouted as he pounded on the door to the cabin, which was really no more than a dugout built into the side of a small hill. "Open up in there!"

The door opened a crack, and a rifle barrel was shoved into Bat's face. "Who's asking?" a rough voice crackled.

"It's Bat Masterson, you old skunk. We're half frozen out here."

The door opened, and a short, wiry man with an enormous gray-flecked beard motioned for them to enter. Harry Lovell was dressed in a red flannel shirt and a pair of long johns. Bat had Kinch carry Josh over to the fire. "We'll need to warm him up some," Bat said. Insulated by several feet of snow, the little dugout was warm and cozy inside. Bat leaned his face close to the fire.

"That's a sure way to tell a greenhorn from a feller who's had him a winter or two," Lovell crackled, watching the ice melt from Bat's mustache. "I remember the first time I had a froze-up mustache like that. I tried to break the ice off! Why, I walked around with only half a mustache for a couple of months after that!"

After Bat had thawed out, he explained to Lovell about Dave Rudabaugh and his gang.

"He's been here before," Lovell said. "So he knows how to find the place. But maybe we oughtta send up a flag for him."

"What do you have in mind?" asked Bat.

"Well," said Lovell, "there's a brush pile outside I've been using for kindlin'. You go out and set it afire. That'll bring anybody within a few miles."

Bat smiled and nodded. "That just might work."

"Sure it will work!" said Lovell. "Meanwhile, I'll brew up some tea for your sick friend there."

Josh groaned. "Sorry I ain't gonna be much help to you, Sheriff. I'm just plumb tuckered out."

"We can handle it, Josh," said Bat. "You just rest up a spell."

Outside, Bat pulled the heavy blanket off the brush pile and set it ablaze with a torch. The twigs crackled and sputtered. Suddenly bright orange flames leaped up, and hundreds of sparks went twisting high into the night sky. When Bat returned to the warmth of the cabin, Lovell was just feeding Josh some of his home-brewed remedy.

"You were right," Bat said to Lovell. "That pile went up nice and bright. Anybody within ten miles can see it." Turning to Kinch he said, "I hate to point this out, friend, but we'd better wait out in the barn."

Kinch sighed. He had his big backside tilted cozily toward the fire. "You're right, Bat. Rudabaugh may be an outlaw, but he'll still put up his horses before he comes looking for Lovell's hospitality." He shook his head sadly. "Darn his hide."

"You fellers watch out now," warned Lovell. "Rudabaugh's one of them grizzly bears you'll have to plug two or three times before he'll go down. I'll keep a watch from in here, too."

Bat and Kinch checked their guns—which could get cranky and misfire in the damp and cold—then pushed their way outside. Where the brush pile had burned there was now only a dark, smoldering puddle. "I sure hope them boys had a chance to see the fire," Bat said. "Well," he told Kinch resignedly, "let's get settled in the barn."

For the next two hours Bat stood shivering, his eyes

glued to a peephole between two boards that opened out onto the snow-covered clearing. The moon cast a narrow ribbon of light on the snow. Bat was beginning to doze when he heard the faintest jingle of a spur. "Kinch," he whispered, "they're here." Kinch scrambled to his feet, and both men readied their guns as they took their positions on either side of the barn door. They could hear the muffled voices of Rudabaugh and his men as they dismounted.

Just then the heavy barn door was heaved open, and Dave Rudabaugh himself stepped inside. Covered in a heavy buffalo robe that was topped with a layer of snow, Rudabaugh appeared in the reflected moonlight as fearsome as a distempered grizzly. His long black mustache and beard were encrusted with ice.

Suddenly Kinch threw back the shade on a lantern, and Bat stepped into the light.

"Hands up!" he shouted. "You're all covered." His rifle was leveled at Rudabaugh. "Rudabaugh, let's have that pistol."

Rudabaugh blinked and took a step back. He gingerly dropped his gun onto the ground.

"Good grief, Masterson," said Rudabaugh as he lifted the heavy buffalo robe from his shoulders. "You didn't have to get all spiffed up just to arrest me."

Bat had taken off his overcoat to free up his movements, so he stood there in his fancy black long-tailed suit coat with striped pants and neatly combed hair and mustache. At his side hung his silver-mounted pearl-handled Colt. In the middle of this winter wasteland, the dapper sheriff was about as unlikely a sight as could be expected.

Suddenly Rudabaugh heaved the buffalo robe at Kinch. From outside, his six partners began firing wildly into the open doorway. Bat stood his ground and pumped his Winchester three times, each shot raising one of the silhouetted figures off his horse.

Rudabaugh then flung himself at Bat, pummeling him with his fists. Kinch, who had been knocked backward by the big buffalo robe, was rushed by one of Rudabaugh's men. Kinch grabbed his gun by the barrel and swung it hard. The outlaw was laid out flat.

"Hang in there, Bat!" Kinch yelled. He swung again and brought the gun down across Rudabaugh's back. Rudabaugh hardly flinched. He rose up from where he had Bat pinned, and he backhanded Kinch, spinning him against the wall. Big Kinch slumped to the floor.

Bat had only a second to catch his breath before Rudabaugh was on him again. Bat reached for his revolver, but Rudabaugh slapped it away like a grizzly would slap a trout out of a stream. Bat was thrown backward into the dirt. Rudabaugh smiled. "It looks to be the end of the road for you, Masterson," he said.

Just then shots rang out from the dugout. Rudabaugh turned his head for a moment. Bat reached for his cane in the dirt and swung for all he was worth. Rudabaugh grunted, straightened up, then fell on top of the sheriff like a poleaxed cow.

A few minutes later Lovell and Josh came to the door of the barn. Their rifles were anchored into the backs of two more outlaws.

"Sheriff Masterson? Bat?" called out Josh. "Are you shot?"

"No, I ain't shot," came a muffled voice from somewhere beneath the unconscious figure of Dave Rudabaugh. "But I'm likely to be dead anyway if you don't get this grizzly bear off me!"

When Bat and his posse got back to Dodge City with their prisoners, a crowd led them to the railroad depot, where a special boxcar was waiting on the siding. It was one of the iron-barred buffalo cars that Buffalo Bill Cody had ordered for his new Wild West theatrical. Two U.S. marshals helped Bat march Rudabaugh and his gang into the car, then slammed and locked the iron bars.

"Bill Cody sent the car out here for some buffalo," one of the marshals told Bat, "so we decided to get a little extra use out of it!"

"Well, what you've got there's no buffalo," laughed Bat. "But it's sure as heck a grizzly bear."

CHARLIE SIRINGO

Charles A. Siringo was born in Texas in 1855. By the age of four-teen he was a working cowboy, driving herds up the Chisholm Trail. In 1885 he published his first autobiography, A Texas Cow Boy, or Fifteen Years on the Hurricane Deck of a Spanish Pony. After that Siringo worked for twenty-two years as a cowboy detective for the Pinkerton National Detective Agency, tracking rustlers, train robbers, bank robbers, and other outlaws.

From 1899 to 1902, Siringo helped track Butch Cassidy and the Sundance Kid—a trail that led him over twenty-five thousand miles, mostly on horseback. This is the story of Charlie Siringo's first dealings with Butch Cassidy and his gang, the Wild Bunch.

Cowboy Detective

We've got to plan this carefully, boys," said W. A. Pinkerton. "Butch Cassidy is as smart as any criminal I've ever run into. And as dangerous!"

From the back of the room, Detective Charlie Siringo nodded in agreement. At forty-four, Charlie was the oldest detective of the dozen or so gathered that day in the Denver office of the Pinkerton National Detective Agency. He sat with his long legs stretched out in front of him. Having spent most of his life in a saddle, Charlie was so bowlegged that standing in one place for very long pained him. And he had been through so many of Mr. Pinkerton's long-winded briefings that the mere sound of his voice was enough to make Charlie's legs ache.

Jim Staggs, a young detective who had just come west with Pinkerton from Chicago, spoke up next. "I read in the newspaper that Cassidy has never killed a man in his life. If that's true, can he really be as dangerous as you say?"

Pinkerton smiled, then scratched his freshly shaved chin. A Chicago businessman by trade, he looked out of place in Denver with his fancy suit and trim mustache. But every man in the room, including Charlie Siringo, respected his intelligence. As president of the Pinkerton National Detective Agency, he ran the best private police and investigation outfit in the country.

"Jim, I'll tell you two things. First, Butch Cassidy's gang includes at least fifty outlaws who are killers. Second, just because he doesn't kill bank tellers and stage drivers doesn't mean that he wouldn't downright enjoy leaving a trail of dead Pinkerton men."

Pinkerton directed his detectives' attention to a map on the wall. "Look at this. You all know about Cassidy's activities before he was jailed in 1894. Back then he was known as Robert Parker, and he robbed stagecoaches with Bill McCarty, who used to run with Jesse James." Pinkerton turned away from the map. "Charlie Siringo, in the back there, helped track down James in New Mexico. I'm sure he can tell you just how bad a crew of outlaws we're talking about here."

Siringo nodded. "They ain't gotten any nicer just 'cause they moved north," he explained. "After Cassidy got out of jail a few years back he did the first thing a young, enterprising outlaw would do: he formed up his own gang, called the Wild Bunch. And gentlemen, 'wild' is the right word. This is going to be a rough show, and no doubt about it."

The other detectives in the room nodded solemnly.

"Last month," Pinkerton said, "the Wild Bunch allegedly robbed the paymaster at the Castle Gate Mine—here." Mr. Pinkerton tapped the map with a pointer. "Less than a week later, near Wilcox, Wyoming, they reportedly blew up the express car of the Union Pacific's Overland Flyer. They

made off with thirty thousand dollars in cash." Pinkerton looked gravely at his detectives. "They also killed a sheriff."

Jim Staggs shifted uncomfortably in his chair. He looked about the room, wondering who among them might be killed next. It was an awful, sobering thought.

"There have been several small bank robberies as well," Pinkerton continued, "here, and here, and here." His pointer swept over huge portions of Colorado, Wyoming, and Montana. Even a detective as inexperienced as Jim noticed immediately that the crime scenes were hundreds of miles apart.

"In each robbery," Pinkerton explained, "the victim was always in possession of large amounts of cash. In other words," Pinkerton concluded, "Cassidy has advance information about who to rob . . . and exactly when."

Charlie Siringo leaned forward in his chair and stared at the map. The puzzle, Charlie understood, was figuring out how the Wild Bunch relayed information back and forth across so many miles so quickly.

"Cassidy and his boys are kicking up dust all over the territory," Pinkerton observed gravely.

"It's too bad we can't just follow Butch's dust cloud around," Charlie joked.

Everyone laughed, including Pinkerton. Then he turned serious again.

"Men, you'll be going up against a very well organized network of outlaws. Remember, what we need most is information on how they operate. No one expects you to collar the whole gang. Good luck."

When the meeting broke up, Charlie left the office with Jim Staggs tagging along at his elbow. To Jim, the older detective was a real-life hero. In fact, just about everyone knew about the famous Charlie Siringo. Back in Chicago, Jim had read Siringo's book about being a Texas cowboy, and he had loved every wild word of it. Now he decided that he would hang on to the famous cowboy detective like a bear to a honey tree.

"Do you have any plans yet, Mr. Siringo?" Jim asked, hardly able to contain his excitement. "Can I come along with you? I'm sure I can learn a lot if you let me join up with you."

Charlie stopped, then looked Jim up and down. "Well now," he said, rubbing his chin. "That's a certainty." He smiled. "Okay, I reckon you can join me. But you'll learn more by watchin' than by talkin'."

Jim took the hint. He would observe Charlie and ask questions only when it was important. But he couldn't help grinning from ear to ear.

The first thing Charlie did was to sell his fancy saddle and silver bridle. At a secondhand clothing store, Charlie bought an old, worn-out Mexican sombrero, a tattered pair of chaps, and a pair of boots that Jim thought looked as bad as if they had been trampled by a stampede.

"Here, kid," Charlie said, handing Jim a second pair of boots that, if possible, were in even worse shape than Charlie's. "Put these on," he instructed.

Back at his hotel, Charlie dug into his trunk and came up with a couple of old trail-worn flannel shirts.

"It's a disguise!" Jim said, finally catching on. "Who are you supposed to be?"

"I am what I've always been. I'm a stove-up old cowpuncher who's spent a lifetime on the hurricane deck of a cow pony. If I run into old Butch, I'll let on that I had some trouble down Texas way. Maybe I killed a feller over a saloon girl. Or maybe I killed me a Texas Ranger. Let's see, I'll need a name, too."

"Mr. Pinkerton told me to always keep my own first name when I'm in disguise," Jim said.

"That's right," Charlie said. "That way you don't turn your head if you hear somebody call out 'Jim' when you're supposed to be a Tom or a George. I'll be Charlie . . . Carter."

The next day the two Pinkertons headed north. Jim and Charlie looked to all the world like a pair of broken-down, hard-on-their-luck cowboy drifters.

Their final destination was Hole-in-the-Wall, Wyoming, the notorious headquarters and hideout of the Wild Bunch and other gangs. From Denver, Jim and Charlie followed the South Platte River north to Greeley, then struck northwest across the plains in an unbroken trek until they reached Laramie, Wyoming. There they spent a couple of days "whooping 'er up."

The reason for that, Charlie explained to Jim when they were back on the trail, was simple. "If you want to be taken for an outlaw, you've got to live like one. We're in Cassidy's territory, now," Charlie said. "Anyone back there could have been an informant for him."

"But how would an informant way down in Laramie get word so quickly to Cassidy all the way up in Hole-in-the-Wall?" asked Jim.

"That's what we're here to find out," Charlie said. "We'll put in similar appearances in Medicine Bow and Casper and maybe Kaycee, too. We'll just keep on until we run into someone who knows something."

"You seem to know this country pretty well," Jim remarked.

"I've ridden this trail a dozen times in my life," Charlie said, then laughed. "But this sure is the only time I ever got paid for stopping in each saloon along the way!"

The ride from Denver to Kaycee took about twelve days. In that time they covered nearly 270 miles and stopped in at least a half-dozen saloons. But so far they hadn't come across any acquaintances of Butch Cassidy.

In Kaycee, a little cow town about thirty miles east of Hole-in-the-Wall, they finally met up with Lonny Logan, a member of the Wild Bunch. Lonny was the older brother of Kid Curry, the deadliest killer of all the outlaws in the Wild Bunch.

Charlie and Lonny hit it off right away. They traded tales of outlaw deeds, gambling, and drinking. Charlie impressed Jim as a natural-born storyteller. He never seemed to be at a loss for "just one more." Jim admired the way Charlie played his role as a cowpoke on the run from Texas. Jim's role in the charade was to play the part of Charlie's orphaned young nephew.

"Uncle Charlie is going to teach me to be a train robber," Jim told Lonny. "We're headed up to Hole-in-the-Wall to join the Wild Bunch and meet Mr. Cassidy. He's been a hero of mine from way back."

"You ain't old enough to have a 'way back,' kid,"

laughed Lonny. "But if you want to meet Butch, I can take you to him."

The next day they hit the trail. Instead of heading for Hole-in-the-Wall, however, Lonny turned north up the Outlaw Trail toward Landusky, Montana. The weather was sunny and mild, and Jim could not help but enjoy the scenery. To their right were mountains, and to their left, the green rolling hills that swept away as far as the eye could see. Along the Bighorn River the wildflowers were in full riot and the meadows were teeming with game.

Having grown up among the congested tenements of Chicago, Jim thought this was about as beautiful a place as any on earth. He only wished they could have made this visit under more pleasant circumstances. He suddenly remembered the dead sheriff from the holdup. Jim grew somber when he realized that it could have been Lonny Logan who pulled the trigger.

Landusky was a tiny Montana cow town of fewer than a half-dozen unpainted, windblown buildings. There was a telegraph office, a general store, a blacksmith, and a few houses scattered on either side of the dirt main street. The men dismounted in front of Jake's Eatery & Saloon. Seated inside, at a table near the door, was Butch Cassidy, the most famous outlaw alive.

"Well, who's this?" Cassidy asked.

Charlie smiled politely as Lonny explained to Cassidy how the two men had stumbled into the bar in Kaycee. Butch Cassidy was a short man, wide at the shoulders and narrow at the hips, with sandy brown hair and a short bushy mustache. He had pale blue eyes and a short scar on one cheek.

"The name's Charlie Carter," said Charlie, extending his hand to Cassidy. "I had me a little run-in with a ranger down in Texas, and me and the boy here decided to hightail it north." Charlie shook his head, amused. "This ranger tracked me all the way from Waco to the panhandle of Texas! He seemed to think I had a little bit too much cash in my saddlebags, so he tried to arrest me." Charlie paused, then said with a chuckle, "He should have shot me first and *then* arrested me."

"You killed yourself a Texas Ranger?" asked Cassidy.

"I'm afraid so," said Charlie in his slow drawl. He nodded toward Jim. "That's when I fetched Jimmy here away from his stepfather. The skunk was working the poor kid like a mule." Charlie looked appealingly at Cassidy. "I'd heard about how well you was doing up here, so we headed on north."

Butch looked blankly at Charlie, then turned his attention to Jim. "So I'm one of your heroes, kid? It seems a darned fool thing to do to make a hero out of a train robber. What have you got to say for yourself, kid?"

Jim had his speech well prepared. "Gosh, Mr. Cassidy," Jim said, "you're the Robin Hood of the West. That's what a newspaper called you once. Everybody says you never killed anyone and that you're a good friend to the working cowboy." He looked down shyly for a second, then continued. "I reckon half the fellers I grew up with wanted to be like you!"

Cassidy stared at him for a long minute. Jim had expected his eyes to be cold and mean looking, but Cassidy's pale blue eyes were not at all as Jim had imagined. In fact, there was even a humorous twinkle in them. "Hear that, boys?" said Cassidy, chuckling. "Some folks think I'm the devil himself, but Jim-boy here thinks I'm Robin Hood. Life do get strange, don't it?"

The men gathered around the table laughed. The group included Kid Curry, Elza Lay, Bob Meeks, Deaf Charley Hanks, and a dozen others that Charlie didn't immediately recognize. What he *did* notice was that each man packed two revolvers. Some also had long knives hanging at their belts or sheathed in their boots.

They ain't exactly dressed for going to church, now, are they? Charlie asked himself, and chuckled.

"What's so funny?" Cassidy asked him.

"Nothin'," Charlie said. "Nothin' at all."

For the next several days, Charlie and Jim just hung around Landusky, doing a little hunting and fishing, having shooting matches, and talking with the "boys" in Jake's tavern. But mostly they waited. Charlie told Jim that Cassidy would take his time deciding if they could join his gang and that they should be patient. The thing to do for the time being was to act natural.

"We're doing our job just fine," Charlie told Jim when the younger detective began to act fidgety. "Remember, we're here to learn how they operate, not to collar the whole gang. So far we don't know much more than we did the day we arrived."

One afternoon Lonny ran into Jake's with a telegraph

message for Cassidy. There were only six other men in the tavern, including Charlie. Cassidy read the message and smiled.

"Big Nose and his boys pulled off a good one down in Colorado," Cassidy crowed. "They swiped more than twenty thousand dollars from the bank!" The men cheered. So did Charlie, but not before he noticed that Cassidy had crumpled up the message, put it in the ashtray, and put a match to it.

"What you got going, Butch?" Charlie asked. He wanted to sound curious, but not *too* curious. "Trains here, banks there, and you never getting out of that chair. I got to admire your organization!"

"I call it the Train Robbers Syndicate," Cassidy said in a polished, "highfalutin' " accent. "Of course, banks are included."

Charlie smiled appreciatively. Butch Cassidy had just made his first mistake.

Later that day Charlie took Jim fishing in the cold waters of Cow Creek, about ten miles from Landusky. Charlie wanted a place where he and Jim could talk without being overheard. Charlie filled Jim in on his discovery.

"If they can talk to each other over the telegraph," Charlie explained, "it can mean one of two things. Either they've bought off a whole lot of telegraph operators all over three states, or they've got a code."

"They've got the money to do the first," said Jim. He frowned. "But it seems unlikely."

Charlie agreed. "That would mean bribing railroad men, postal clerks, telegraph operators, and a lot of others. It *could* be done, I suppose, but there would be a lot of risk in it. And Butch Cassidy is too smart for that." Charlie shook his head.

"Different branches of the gang must be scattered all over. Some are robbers, and some are just informants. They must be using a code to talk to each other over the public telegraph wires." Charlie suddenly looked straight at Jim. "I'll bet you that even the telegraph operator in Landusky doesn't know what the messages mean!"

"Just knowing that there's a code doesn't help much," said Jim. "Does it?"

"It helps," Charlie said. "You see, the code couldn't be too out of the ordinary or the telegraph operators would have noticed it themselves. I'll bet they've figured out a way to make it read like normal messages." Jim appeared confused. Charlie smiled. "Okay. It might be something like 'Nelly's getting married at Saturday at nine,' which might mean that '*Saturday*, the number *nine* train is carrying a lot of cash,' or something like that."

Jim nodded. "So what do we do?" he asked.

"I reckon we ought to make a midnight visit to a certain telegraph office," Charlie said. "Telegraph operators are required to keep records of all their messages in a logbook. If I can get a look at some of those messages, maybe I can break the code. Then we'll just wire the information to Denver."

"I suppose using a telegraph key is another of your talents?" asked Jim.

"It's come in handy before," answered Charlie.

"But why go at midnight?" Jim asked. "Why couldn't we just walk in and demand to read the logs?"

"Too risky," Charlie said. "I can't be one-hundred-percent positive the telegraph operator isn't one of Cassidy's men. Now, let's get back to Landusky with these trout. I'm getting hungry."

Two nights later Charlie made his midnight visit to the telegraph office. The moon was full, so he did not need to light a candle inside the office to read the logbook. Just as he thought, the book contained all the messages that had come in or gone out of Landusky over the past year.

Charlie read painstakingly through all the messages, right down to one that had come in that very afternoon. "Next Thursday," read the final entry, "you pay up at Tipton. Meet you at ten at the bridge." Charlie recognized the phrase "you pay" from other messages and figured it was the code for the "U.P.," the Union Pacific train.

"The train must be coming through Tipton at ten o'clock," Charlie mumbled to himself, "and his gang means to rob it at some bridge."

Charlie immediately tapped out a message to Pinkerton in the Denver office.

Hidden in the shadows outside the office, Jim kept watch. He jumped nervously when he heard the hammering of the telegraph key. The click-click-click went on and on. By the time Charlie was finished, Jim seemed as shaky as a leaf in a windstorm.

"What took you so long?" Jim asked.

"Come on, Jim," Charlie whispered, "let's get some sleep. We'll most likely be in the saddle early tomorrow."

That morning, just as Charlie hoped, Cassidy invited him and Jim to join a "little party" they were going to "down

Tipton way." Of course, they accepted. Along the trail they were joined by four more members of the gang. Cassidy explained that Charlie and Jim, being new to the train-robbing business, would guard their escape route, a half mile back from the railroad tracks.

First, Charlie and Jim helped the gang pile logs across the tracks.

"Good luck!" Charlie called out as he and Jim prepared to ride out.

"Luck has nothing to do with it!" answered Cassidy confidently.

"We'll see about that," Charlie muttered under his breath.

Back in the woods Charlie and Jim waited for the Union Pacific train to pull into view.

Charlie reached into his saddlebag and pulled out a pair of binoculars. "Ha!" he laughed. "Looks like Mr. Pinkerton has prepared a little surprise for Butch." He handed Jim the binoculars. "Take a look."

All along the length of the train, from the engineer's cabin back to the caboose, Jim saw dozens of Pinkerton men with rifles, standing on the side of the train. Jim smiled. "It looks like Butch Cassidy's luck has just run out."

"Why, Jim," Charlie said, grinning, "luck has nothing to do with it!"

WILD BILL HICKOK

James Butler Hickok, better known as Wild Bill, was born in 1837 in Troy Grove, Illinois. At the age of seventeen he headed west to join the irregular army of Kansas Free-Staters who were fighting the Missouri mobs who wanted to turn the Kansas territory into a slave state. Later, Hickok worked as a teamster on the Santa Fe Trail, where he met Buffalo Bill Cody. Both of them worked for the Pony Express until Hickok joined the Union Army as a scout when the Civil War broke out. After the war Hickok continued scouting, mainly fighting Sioux with the Seventh and Tenth Cavalry regiments. By this time Hickok was already famous because of several articles that had been written about his exploits, naming him the Prince of Pistoleers. In 1869, Wild Bill became the sheriff of Hays City, Kansas, the roughest town on the frontier at that time. In 1871 the marshal of Abilene, Tom Smith, was murdered. The mayor of Abilene asked Hickok to become the four-year-old city's new marshal.

Prince of Pistoleers

ames Butler Hickok cut a startling figure as he rode into
the dusty cow town of Abilene, Kansas. He wore check-
ered trousers and a fancy black frock coat with long tails.
On his head was a low-crowned, wide-brimmed black hat with
a silver-studded hatband. His long chestnut hair fell to his
shoulders, and his thick mustache trailed down to his jaw.
Hickok's picture had appeared so often in so many newspapers
from New York to California that he was recognized immediately almost everywhere he went. Abilene was no exception.

It was only a little after sunup on that spring morning in
1871, yet most of Abilene was already up, and the town was
bustling with activity. As Hickok turned down the wide dirt
avenue called Texas Street, however, everyone stopped what
they were doing and turned to stare.

A boy with tousled red hair ran out into the street.

"Are you Wild Bill Hickok?" the boy asked.

"I've been known to answer to that name, son," Hickok
drawled. "Could you tell me where I might find the mayor?"

"Yes sir, Mr. Hickok!" the boy shouted, and pointed.
"Head on down Texas Street, then go to the end of Railroad
Street. You'll see the sign."

Hickok thanked the boy and rode on, but he could hear the townsfolk gossiping as he passed. "That's Wild Bill!" one man said to his friend. "He's come to take Tom Smith's place," another speculated. "There goes the Prince of Pistoleers," gushed a third.

Hickok had to smile. Newspaper reporters had dubbed him Wild Bill Hickok, Prince of Pistoleers. The reporters claimed that he had killed more than a hundred men in gunfights. Hickok knew that that was a wild exaggeration. He had killed only two men in his career as a lawman, but the reputation had more than once deterred a would-be gunfighter from picking a fight with him.

The mayor's office was a bit fancier than the others Hickok had seen in frontier towns. But it wasn't Mayor McCoy's swivel chair or big rolltop desk that impressed Hickok. It was that the sign out front had no bullet holes in it. The former marshal, Tom Smith, had done a good job of taming Abilene.

Mayor McCoy almost jumped out of his chair to greet Hickok, shaking his hand vigorously as he spoke.

"Honored to meet you, Mr. Hickok," he said. "I take it you've accepted our offer to be the new marshal here?"

Hickok was amused by the way the little man's bristling red eyebrows worked up and down while his tiny trimmed mustache hardly moved.

As a rule Hickok respected these frontier mayors. Mayoring might be a harder job even than marshaling, he thought. After all, he figured, a six-gun and a silver star earned a man a measure of respect that mayors didn't get.

"Call me Bill," he said, taking a seat opposite the desk.

"And you take it correctly. I'm here for the job, though the town looks a lot calmer than stories make it out to be."

"Don't be fooled, Bill," said Mayor McCoy. "It looks peaceful enough now, but by the middle of June this town will be overrun with rowdy Texas cowboys. Their pockets will be full of cash, and each one of them will be bent on raising seven kinds of ruckus. By summer's end, when all the herds have been shipped out on the rails, seven thousand Texans will have come and gone."

"Sounds just like Hays City," said Hickok, "but I managed to settle down that cow town. Tell me what you want done and I'll see to it."

"Fine," McCoy said. "There's a 'No Gun' law in town that's got to be enforced. You'll need to keep an eye out for crooked card games, too. More men get killed over card games than anything else. But there's one more thing," he said as two deputies walked in. One deputy was Tom Carson, the nephew of the famous mountain man Kit Carson, and the other was James MacDonald.

Hickok nodded to them both, then turned back to the mayor. "You were saying?"

"We're not dead certain just who killed Marshal Smith last summer. It may have just been the locals that we arrested, but there may have been others involved, too. The fact is, by agreeing to become marshal of Abilene you might just as well be wearing a target on your shirt as a badge."

"Don't worry," said Hickok, rising from his chair. "Being so well known, I've gotten used to the notion that every young buck with a fast hand thinks he has to mix it up with old Wild Bill. Some have tried. None have succeeded."

Mayor McCoy laughed and handed Hickok a silver marshal's star. "I'm mighty pleased to welcome you to Abilene, Mr. Hickok."

Hickok and his deputies spent the next two months preparing for the arrival of the Texas cattle herds. They put up new signs at each end of town to remind the cowboys that all guns were to be checked in at the marshal's office or at the door of any hotel or saloon. They put a new roof on the jail, too. A cowboy had lassoed a beam the previous summer and almost succeeded in having his pony pull the roof off. As a further precaution, they nailed a second layer of boards on the walls of the jail.

"This way," Hickok told his deputies, "if some cowboy takes it into his head to shoot up the jail, he won't do no real harm."

When Hickok was not busy fortifying the town against the coming onslaught of cowboys, he often entertained the children with stories about his days working for the Pony Express, or about fighting Indians with the cavalry, or about being a marshal in other cow towns.

It was on just such an afternoon in early May that the children turned away from one of Hickok's stories and began pointing excitedly to the south. "The Texans are coming! The Texans are coming!" they shouted.

A dark cloud of dust that was blotting out the pale blue sky had formed on the horizon. Cattle herds were coming up the Chisholm Trail.

"No more afternoons like this one for a spell," Hickok said to himself as he followed the children back into town.

He was right. Abilene changed overnight. By the next evening the streets were overflowing with rowdy cowboys.

Squealing fiddles, tinny pianos, Texas whoops, and coarse laughter filled the air. Hickok braced himself for trouble. He didn't have long to wait.

At the Novelty Theater, a group of cowboys decided it would be fun to dance onstage. They noisily cleared the room by throwing most of the tables and chairs through the windows. The cowboys then stomped around the room like a stampeding herd of cattle as the music swelled louder and louder.

Hickok and his deputies casually stepped through one of the broken windows. Tom Carson stayed at the door, and James MacDonald climbed onto the stage. Marshal Hickok then strode purposefully across the crowded room and kicked the stool out from under the piano player, silencing the music. He raised his pistol into the air and fired three shots. The dancing cowboys suddenly dived for the floor.

"Don't one of you varmints move a muscle!" Hickok ordered. "Now, one at a time, let's all line up at the door like good little cowboys. You're all going to spend the night at the Hotel Hickok."

It was a bit cramped in the two-cell jail that night—and for many nights after.

But one citizen of Abilene was not happy with the new marshal. Phil Coe, the owner of the Bull's Head Saloon, was angry that under Hickok's watchful eye, Coe's crooked gambling operation was losing money. As the summer wore on, Coe grew to hate Hickok, who often sat at one of the back tables of the Bull's Head, observing the games.

Coe finally had had enough. Watching his losses mount,

Coe instructed his dealers to resume cheating whenever the marshal wasn't around.

It wasn't long before the cowboys were complaining to Mayor McCoy about the loaded dice and extra aces at the Bull's Head.

"You've got to keep them games honest, Marshal," McCoy told Hickok one afternoon. "Otherwise, there's going to be some serious violence." McCoy leaned forward in his chair. "If the cowboys take a disliking to our hospitality," he explained, "next year they might drive their cattle to some other railhead. We couldn't afford that. Without the cattle business, Abilene would be a ghost town.

"We're talking about the life of a town here, Marshal. One day we'll be a city. We can't do anything to jeopardize that. It's a thin line we've got to walk. We've got to keep them cowboys happy, but you've also got to keep them from busting up the town."

"It's all right, Mayor," Hickok said, reassuring him. "I've walked that line before."

That evening Hickok slipped in the back door of the Bull's Head and sat down to watch the games. It was only a few minutes before everyone in the place knew that the marshal was there, but in that short time Hickok had spotted some crooked play. He walked up to where Coe sat dealing cards in a game of faro, and he leaned over the table. "Enough's enough, Coe," he said. "I'm closing this place down."

Coe's gray eyes glittered like a sidewinder's, cold and calculating. "You can't close me down," he warned Hickok. "This town needs citizens like me. *Taxpaying* citizens. Go mind your own business, Marshal."

Hickok's right hand whipped out his long-barreled Colt,

which twirled twice around his finger before slapping into his palm. The muzzle was one inch from Coe's ear. The crowd behind Coe pushed back in panic. It didn't pay to be in Wild Bill Hickok's line of fire.

"You're dead wrong about this town needing you," Hickok said. "Abilene needs scum like you about like it needs a cholera epidemic." He cocked the silver pistol. The sound was heard by everyone in the saloon. "You try to open your doors tomorrow, Coe, and I'll personally come down and nail them shut. And I wouldn't mind nailing your mangy hide up over the door, either."

Hickok turned to the crowd. "Cash in your chips, boys. The Bull's Head is history."

That night Coe began plotting his revenge. Neither cowboys nor saloon girls could keep secrets very well, so by next morning Hickok had a pretty good idea what Phil Coe was planning. In fact, Coe had even begun bragging about what he was going to do to that "longhaired fancy-dressing son of a mule."

Two nights later Hickok was sitting by the window in the Alamo Saloon and Restaurant, sipping strong black coffee as he did every night before he went on his rounds. A pretty, green-eyed waitress was just about to pour him a second cup when gunfire erupted down the street. Hickok pushed back his chair and jumped to his feet. "Go ahead and pour that coffee," he told her, winking. "I'll be back shortly."

A small crowd had gathered in the middle of Texas Street. It was a moonless night, but the light from the saloon windows was thrown in long yellow rectangles on the ground all along the street. Phil Coe was at the front of the crowd, gun in hand.

"Coe!" Hickok shouted as he strode toward the crowd. "Put that gun down before somebody gets hurt. You know the law!"

"I ain't some drunken cowboy you can bully!" Coe sneered. "I'm a citizen, and I got a right to carry whatever I want." He turned so that the gun in his hand was pointed at Hickok. It was already cocked. "You come any closer," he warned Hickok, "and I'm going to be just about as famous as you are." Coe grinned meanly. "I won't mind being the man who killed Wild Bill Hickok."

"I'm going to count to three," Hickok said matter-of-factly, "and that six-gun better be back in its holster."

Just then two rifle shots blazed from a nearby rooftop. Hickok could feel the impact of the rifle slugs in the dirt just inches from his boots. His right hand flicked to his gun, and he fired once at the spot where the rifleman was hiding on the roof.

At the same time, Coe aimed his gun. "It's my turn now, Hickok!" Coe snarled, and he fired. The bullet whizzed harmlessly through the folds of Hickok's wide frock coat. Another grazed the inside of one thigh.

Hickok stood motionless and calmly dropped Coe with a single shot. A second later the body of the rifleman rolled off the roof, thudding heavily onto the street.

"Clean up this mess before morning, boys," Hickok said to the men standing around with their hands in their pockets. "Abilene's a clean town. While I'm marshal, there'll be no crooked card games, no guns, and no bodies littering the streets."

At the Alamo restaurant, the green-eyed waitress smiled as she handed Hickok his coffee.